A Little Bit of Murder

Short mysteries to confuse and amuse

Doodlebug Press

ISBN-978-0-6151-9132-4

Dedication

These stories are dedicated to all of the mystery fans out there who enjoy figuring out whodunit. I would also like to acknowledge my husband Robert and my daughter Mya who have been more than patient with me as I spend hours at my computer dreaming up stories like these.

Introduction

A Little Bit of Murder is a collection of short murder mysteries written as part of a contest held at the author's blog. The solutions to the mysteries presented here are given at the back of the book. See if you can guess what happened without looking at the answers! Go ahead, have some fun!

With One Stone

Marla Franzen volunteers at the local bird sanctuary. She's been there for five years and she absolutely loves her work. Recently, there's been talk that the sanctuary will be closing. The rumor is that a local developer wants to buy the land so that he can build a community of condominiums. Funding hasn't exactly been great for the sanctuary and the board of trustees for the organization has voted to consider selling the property. Marla has been extremely vocal on the topic and has made it clear on a number of occasions that this is not an acceptable course of action. After all, she says, the community doesn't need another group of condos. The sanctuary is the last peaceful area in town and losing it would be a terrible shame.

Dr. George Ballast, the local dentist is on the board of trustees. He has voted against the sale of the sanctuary each time it has come up in discussion. He is the only one on the board who feels that this would be a great loss to the community. A fellow bird enthusiast, he shares Marla's concerns about adding yet another group of condos to an already over-populated area. His dental assistant, Sheree Harper, is a long-time friend of Marla's and she agrees with the doctor. "It's simply not fair to take away such a beautiful landmark," she says.

Sheriff Robert Winthorp is also a member of the board of trustees. He feels that the sanctuary is not the "haven" that the volunteers tout it to be. The property is poorly maintained and the birds aren't so extraordinary that the community will miss out on anything. Obviously, he is not a bird lover. He's just a member of the board because it was an election year when they recruited him. "We don't even have any parakeets, so why not tear it down," he says.

Local elementary school teacher, Evelyn McInrude, is a board member as well. She claims that the bird sanctuary isn't sustainable and though she hates the idea of letting it go, it isn't practical to try and save it. It isn't a government landmark; it's simply a local project that is failing miserably. The board had never been able to obtain the funding it needed because their grant requests weren't strong enough. For that reason, she maintains that the sanctuary has long been a drain on the board members who have been paying to maintain it thus far.

Tomorrow, the board will vote once more to determine whether or not the contractor's offer is accepted. He's offering $500,000 for the land and the board knows that this is well over market. The problem is that the volunteers, mainly Marla, have organized a sit-in and plan to take action as soon as they board convenes at 9 a.m.

On this particular evening, Marla visits the sanctuary to reminisce about the good times she has had there. The birds are the only thing that kept her sane after she lost her husband of thirty years to cancer. She cries as she walks through the sanctuary and listens to the birds fluttering around. Suddenly, she hears something near the back of the building. Before she knows what is happening, the place is engulfed in flames and she is trapped. She screams, but no one can hear her. No one works here in the evenings and generally, the place is deserted. The fire blazes out of control and it is a long time before the fire trucks arrive.

In the morning, the volunteers arrive to find a charred mess where their sanctuary used to be. The fire trucks are still there and the Fire Marshall is looking around, collecting evidence for his investigation. Most of the board members are in attendance as they are set to meet this morning to vote on the sale of the property. It appears that the vote will now be a no-brainer. Conspicuously absent from the scene are Dr. Ballast, Mrs. McInrude and Marla. The doctor had an emergency extraction and could not attend the meeting this morning. Mrs. McInrude called and left a message saying that she was ill. The other board members decide to discuss the fire once they have convened their meeting.

As they discuss the fire, Sheriff Winthorp asks the board to hold off on the vote out of respect for the loss of the sanctuary. He also mentions that it is curious that all of the volunteers except Marla were present this morning. The board agrees to postpone the vote until the following Monday in order to allow for the appropriate investigations to take place. After all, they had an insurance claim to file and they needed to wait for the inspector's report from the fire department.

A week passes and the Fire Marshall comes to the board's meeting to discuss the findings of his investigation. A female body was found among the ashes and has been identified as Marla Franzen. The board members are shocked and horrified at the news. All but Mrs. McInrude are in attendance and Dr. Ballast confirms what the Fire Marshall says by informing the board that he had to verify the dental records. The body was, in fact, Marla Franzen. No suspects have been identified as the scene was devoid of any usable prints or other evidence. Whoever had burned the sanctuary down had known exactly what they were doing.

Weeks later, there's a break in the case. Dr. Ballast has disappeared and it is reported that he was seen leaving town with a woman at around midnight just hours after the board meeting where the final vote to sell the property had taken place. He and his companion boarded a plane for Costa Rica and it appears that he is not set to return. His office appears to be permanently closed.

The contractor has planned to begin construction of the condominiums within the month and most of the red tape has been dealt with in terms of the insurance claims, etc. Mrs. McInrude never returned to the board meetings and one of the board members took it upon herself to visit McInrude's apartment to make sure she was ok. She found the apartment to be in decent shape, but there was no evidence that McInrude had been there for several weeks.

What is going on here? Who set the fire at the Bird Sanctuary? Who was Dr. Ballast leaving town with? What happened to Mrs. McInrude? **To find out, turn to page 43.**

Board Stiff: A 9 to 5 Mystery

Thornton Westmiller was a prominent executive. He had a corner office, a company car and other perks too numerous to detail. He was also a member of several boards around town. His favorite post was that of Treasurer for a local shelter. One evening, Westmiller received a call at his home from an angry citizen. There were accusations of impropriety and misallocation of funds for the shelter. Annoyed, Westmiller hung up and proceeded to go about his evening ritual of dinner, a few moments of conversation with his lovely wife, Regina, and his usual late night glass of bourbon. He checked over the financial records for the shelter before he went to bed. He had been waiting for funds from a bequest to be transferred into the shelter's account and they hadn't shown up yet. He had figured out a way to "redirect" some of the funds if he could catch the deposit before anyone else noticed it was there. He had been checking it almost hourly for the past couple of days and was starting to get frustrated. He'd give it another day and then he would call his contact to make sure things were going as planned.

The following day, Westmiller received a note at his office along with a nicely wrapped package. Happy to be the recipient of a gift, he anxiously opened the package. But instead of finding a new pair of golf shoes as he had anticipated, he recoiled from the sight of a dead snake with a bright, red ribbon around its broken neck. This gift obviously wasn't from his wife. He opened the note that had come with the package and it said, "The only good snake is a dead snake!" The handwriting was carefully printed in block lettering, no doubt, in order to preserve the sender's anonymity.

He slammed the lid back onto the box and frantically called for his secretary, Judy. She hurried in, her dainty heels clicking across the tile floor.

"What is it, Mr. Westmiller?" she asked. She had only been with the company a short time and wasn't yet familiar with her boss's moods. She assumed he was upset with her for forgetting to make coffee.

"I need you to dispose of this box immediately," he said.

"Dispose, but it's such a beautiful gift," she said, stepping closer to have a look. She lifted the lid and shrieked as she caught sight of its contents. She dropped the lid, stumbled backward and nearly fell right into Westmiller's lap. Thankfully, she caught herself before making contact. She hadn't had any problems with her boss, but he sometimes looked at her in a way that made her a little uncomfortable. She was a beautiful young lady and had left other jobs because her boss's couldn't keep their hands to themselves. She had hoped that Westmiller would be different.

"Just get rid of it," he said.

She scurried away from the desk and called downstairs to the security guard to get some help. Later that day after the box had been removed, Westmiller grudgingly picked up the phone to call the local police. The security guard had suggested that he file a report in case any other crazy packages came for him. "You can never be too careful," he had said.

Since this was a non-emergency call, he was on hold for what seemed like an eternity. As the minutes passed, he decided he could handle this later and hung up the phone. At exactly 5:30 p.m., he packed up his briefcase and headed out of the office. His secretary had already gone, her shift usually ended at 5 p.m. and there was really no reason for her to stay late. He walked past her desk and out of the office, locking the door behind him.

As he made his way through the parking garage, he couldn't stop looking over his shoulder. He was paranoid, and for good reason, who gets a gift-wrapped snake?

He reached his car and looked around the garage one last time before getting into the sleek, new BMW. He started the engine and backed out of the space, then drove off toward downtown. He was on his way to yet another board meeting.

When he reached the parking lot of the Mayfield Family Shelter, he parked close to the building. He was uncharacteristically late for the meeting which had started at 5:30. He walked quickly up the walkway to shelter entrance, stepping carefully over a homeless man who had decided to sit with his legs sprawling out across the narrow path. The man looked like a heap of dirty laundry and smelled just as pleasant. Westmiller looked back, taking in the sight and shaking his head.

He pulled on the door to the shelter and found it locked. He had never been late for a meeting before and hadn't realized that they locked the doors to the shelter at 5:30 sharp. There was a small doorbell situated near the door and he reached out to ring it. After a few moments, he stepped closer to the door and peered inside. He couldn't see anything but an empty reception desk. He pulled his cell phone from his pocket and dialed the number for the office. At the same time, he heard the phone on the desk inside begin to ring.

"Damn it!" he said, flipping his phone shut. He turned to walk back to his car and noticed that the homeless man had disappeared. "Good riddance," he murmured to himself as he walked back down the pathway. It was starting to get dark and he wanted to get out of here. There was no sign of anyone hanging around, but he knew that if something happened out here, no one would know until the board meeting ended. The board met in the basement of the building and there was no way they could see or hear what went on outside from where they were. He looked over his shoulder again as he pulled his car keys from his pocket. When he looked back around, he was face to face with Mr. Chandler, the shelter director.

"Whoa, there," he said, "You scared the life out of me."

"Sorry about that," Mr. Chandler said, "I had to run out for a minute. I'm guessing you're here for the meeting?"

"Yes, actually, I was running late and couldn't get in," he said.

"No problem, let's get in there," Chandler said smiling.

The meeting went on for what seemed like hours, though it was really only about forty-five minutes. They discussed budget and when it came time for the treasurer's report, Westmiller gave them the information he had put together and answered questions from the various members. He had gotten so good at fielding their questions; he didn't even have to think about his responses anymore. Towards the end of the meeting, someone piped up and asked, "Whatever happened with that bequest from Mr. Thompson's estate, the doctor who just passed away."

Westmiller shifted in his seat, this was the money he had been putting aside for his "special project." He shuffled through his reports and pretended to be looking for the deposit information, though he knew it wasn't there.

"Well, there's been some kind of glitch with the funds and the estate is claiming that Mr. Thompson only had us down to receive $100,000 and not the $250,000 we were expecting.

The old man at the end of the table, Mr. Swanson stood up abruptly and smacked his hand down on the table. "That's ridiculous! We have been counting on that money and he had said for years that he would make sure that we received $250,000!"

Taken aback by the man's attitude, Westmiller cleared his throat and said, "Well, I'm not sure what happened, but it appears that the estate wasn't as large as what Thompson had originally thought."

"But he had the funds set aside for us for years," Mrs. Terhune, the local librarian said. "I believe his wife said that it was actually written into his will this way."

"I don't know what to tell you," Westmiller said, "I spoke with the attorney for the estate the other day and he said that there were more expenses than expected with Thompson's medical bills and that he was splitting the remaining monies with three charities here in town."

"That's preposterous!" said Swanson. "I don't believe it! How are we supposed to keep operations going if we don't get the funds we're promised?"

"I understand you're upset, but this is really beyond our control," Westmiller replied, "We'll simply have to make do with what we have. We're lucky to receive anything, you know."

The group grew silent at this and then started nodding their heads in agreement. They were lucky to get any funds from private citizens and they all knew this. The meeting adjourned a few moments later and the group made their way outside. As the crowd dispersed, Westmiller got into his car and drove off toward his house. He received a call on his cell phone as he was pulling out of the shelter lot.

"Hello," he said.

"Westmiller, you don't know who you're dealing with," a voice said. It was low and gravelly, but he couldn't tell if it was a man or a woman.

"Who is this?" he demanded.

"Someone who knows what's going on," the voice said. "You'd better make things right or you'll be sorry."

"Who *is* this?" he demanded again. It was too late, the person had hung up and all he was left with was a dial tone.

"This is ridiculous," he said to himself. He flipped the phone closed and slipped it back into his coat pocket. He drove the rest of the way home, thinking about the call. He was a little worried, but figured it was just some crank trying to throw him off balance. He thought for a moment and then called his friend, Estate Attorney, Art Coughley. The phone rang a couple of times and then Art picked up.

"Art," he said, "Thorn, here. Hey, you wouldn't have made that transfer yet, would you?"

"Hey, Thorn, how's it going?" he said, "No, actually, there's a bit of a problem with it. We should get together and talk."

He checked his watch and said, "Well, I'm not quite home yet, I could swing by if you're not busy."

"Yeah, sure, go ahead, I was just working on some papers," he said, "I could use a break."

They hung up and Westmiller headed toward Coughley's house. He stopped at a drive-thru on the way to pick up a sandwich. He hadn't eaten since lunch and was starving. About twenty-five minutes later, he was pulling through a set of wrought-iron gates and up to the beautiful two-story house where Coughley lived alone. He walked up and knocked on the door, expecting to hear footsteps on the marble tiled floors. He heard nothing. He tried the door and found it unlocked. As he walked inside, he turned to go into the den where Art was normally working.

"Art," he called. "Are you here?"

No answer.

He walked into the den and when the desk came into view, he saw that there was blood all over the place. "Art!" he called. Then he realized that Art was not going to answer. Art was lying on the floor, behind the desk with a knife sticking out of his chest. Westmiller gasped and started to reach for the telephone on the desk. He stopped himself as he caught sight of the computer screen. The account for Mr. Thompson was up and it was open to the transfers screen. Not knowing much about the way this particular software worked, Westmiller thought for a moment. It couldn't hurt to make a couple of adjustments.

Within seconds, he had transferred the money into his accounts and wiped the keyboard and mouse clean of his fingerprints. He stood up and reached for the phone to call the police. As he dialed 9-1-1, he heard footsteps in the hallway. He turned just in time to see the gun as it fired three shots into him. His lifeless body fell in a heap, landing on top of Coughley. The two men lay in a bleeding heap behind the desk as the phone receiver dangled uselessly over them.

What happened? Who pulled the trigger? Who killed Art? Why? To find out, turn to page 45.

Dead Weight

Darnell Wooten worked at a local fitness center. He was a personal trainer and was fairly well-liked by his co-workers and clients. Maybe, a little too well-liked by some. He had plans to get a degree in Physical Therapy and go to work for a rehabilitation center. He was just three classes away from graduation when he was found dead in the gym's weight room.

Three months prior, Darnell's clients included a doctor, a college football player, assorted college cheerleaders and the occasional housewife. The nearby university sent plenty of business his way. It had been rumored that Darnell played the field and that he often became romantically involved with his clients. Although he was generally discreet, he'd had his share of confrontations with angry boyfriends and even husbands.

He had been dating a local cheerleader named Betsy Jantzen for the past six months. Before that, he had spent some quality time with the wife of a local attorney. Before that, he had befriended a shy, young art student, Beverly Whitford and a waitress, Darla Hughes, who frequented the gym. Both of whom he dumped without explanation and both of whom were devastated by the breakups.

On one evening, his girlfriend Betsy stopped by to see if he would like to meet her for dinner later. She just happened to see him locked in an embrace with a fellow trainer, Tandi Gershwin. She walked over to him, tapped him on the shoulder and then stood there until he turned around. He broke free from Tandi and when he turned around, he said, "Betsy, hey, what are you doing here?"

"The better question is what the hell are *you* doing here?" she snapped. Tandi backed up a step and turned to lean against the counter.

Darnell grabbed Betsy's hand and walked her away from where they had been standing. "Hey, Tandi's grandmother passed away, I was just consoling her. She's upset." He was smooth and he had a million excuses ready to use at any time. He just hoped that she hadn't been there a few minutes before the hug when he had been flirting and snapping at the straps on Tandi's leotard.

She thought for a moment and then seemed to be okay with what he had said. She asked him about their dinner plans and then went on her merry way, turning to wave at Tandi on her way out. When Betsy had left the parking lot, Darnell went back to Tandi and told her that

Betsy was under a lot of stress and that she had just overreacted. Tandi didn't really care because she had a boyfriend and considered this to be just harmless flirtation. Nonetheless, she agreed to meet with Darnell later that evening after he had dinner with his *family*.

This is how Darnell got through the days. He juggled relationships and made sure everyone thought he was the good guy. In reality, he was a cheater, a liar and a hopeless jerk. Darnell eventually met his match in a woman named Sally Metzger. She was an attractive, albeit overweight, mother of two who came into the gym to work on losing the extra pounds she had gained after her second child was born. She worked with Darnell for close to three months and had made great progress, losing a whopping thirty pounds. By the time she was ready to tell Darnell she no longer needed his services, he had started to notice that she was looking pretty good. The prospect of a new conquest loomed large in his mind. He decided to make his move.

On their regular rotation, Sally was to do a variety of floor exercises and follow it up with nautilus. She was just getting up from doing a series of pushups when Darnell gave her a pat on the rear end. She looked around at him and said, "What was that?" She wasn't angry; in fact, she had been smiling when she said it.

"Oh, nothing," he said, "I'm sorry, my hand must have slipped."

They exchanged a few comments and then agreed that he should come and have a drink with her later. She wasn't married and she had a babysitter for the evening. The met as planned and from there, the affair began. She was, by far, the most intriguing woman Darnell had ever pursued. She was smart and now, after losing the weight, he found her to be amazingly attractive. After a couple of weeks, he decided that he was going to go ahead and dump his girlfriend Betsy. He had only been stringing her along in case things didn't go well with Sally. He decided to call her and tell her on a Thursday evening.

Betsy picked up the phone on the third ring and said, "Hello."

"Betsy, hey, it's me," he said.

"Hey, I wasn't expecting to hear from you today," she said, sounding pleasantly surprised.

"Yeah, well, I wanted to call and talk to you," he said, "I've been doing some thinking."

"About what?" she asked, puzzled at the serious tone in his voice.

"Well, I've been thinking that this just isn't working out, you know," he said.

"What isn't working out?" she asked.

"Us, dating, it's not been going the way I wanted it to," he said, "and I really don't want to drag it out any longer."

"Drag it out!" she shrieked.

"That's what I mean, you're too moody for me and I just don't feel like we'll ever get past it," he said, still maintaining a calm demeanor, "I just want to call it quits and move on. I do wish you the best."

"Now wait a minute…" she was saying and then she heard the dial tone. He had hung up on her. He had broken up with her over the telephone and then topped it all off by hanging up on her before she could respond. She was furious. She hung up the phone and then grabbed her coat and purse from the wall hook on her way out the door. She wasn't going to let him get away with this. When she got into her car, she drove straight over to the gym. He had called her from work, so she knew he would still be there. It was almost closing time and there were only a few cars in the parking lot, none of them familiar to her.

She slipped into the gym unnoticed. No one was at the counter and it appeared that the place was nearly empty. She could hear the sound of weights clanging in the weight room so she decided to head in that direction. He was probably back there trying to impress Tandi with his bench pressing. When she got to the doorway of the weight room, she looked inside and started to say, "Don't bother trying to impress her…"

Before she could get the words out, she gasped at the sight before her. Darnell was lying on the weight bench with a heavy barbell resting on his neck. He wasn't moving and when she went over to try and lift it off of him; she couldn't even move the thing. She ran out to the counter to find help, but there was no one around. The lights had been turned off and it looked like someone had shut the place down at the same moment she had discovered Darnell. She picked up the phone on the counter and dialed 9-1-1. When the paramedics arrived, they pronounced Darnell dead at the scene. Betsy was taken into custody by the police and an investigation ensued…

Who killed Darnell? Why? To find out, turn to page 48.

An Ounce of Prevention

Erika Johnson was a pharmaceutical sales representative. She worked for one of the big names in the pharmaceutical industry and had a large client base that had been built up over the course of five years. She had started out wanting to be a social worker, but when she figured out that she wouldn't be able to make enough money doing social work, she answered an ad in her local paper and the rest was history. As a sales rep, she made good money and she still felt like she would be helping people because she was offering samples of medication which doctors could then pass on to their patients. At least, this was how she rationalized it.

She had just dropped off her usual week's worth of samples to the largest medical group in town and was waiting for the elevator, when she encountered an elderly woman who asked her, "Are you able to give samples to individual patients?"

"Oh, no, ma'am, I'm sorry," she had responded, "I'm not qualified to make the diagnosis required to dispense the samples. You can ask your doctor for samples the next time you're in."

"Well, my doctor won't give me samples, I've asked him," the lady said in a feeble voice, "I can't afford the regular medication and they tell me if I don't take it, I could have a heart attack."

"I'm really sorry, but I just can't," she had said to the woman. She thought for a moment and then asked, "Which doctor is it that you go to?"

"Dr. Reed, up on the third floor," she answered.

"What medication was it that you needed?" Erika had asked.

The lady gave here the names of her medications and Erika had told her that she would check with the doctor to see if he wanted some samples to hand out. The two parted ways with the older woman thanking Erika profusely for making the effort. Erika made a note in her calendar to visit Dr. Reed and then got in her car and drove home.

Although it was a little unusual, Erika called Dr. Reed's office and asked if she could speak with the doctor regarding a patient of his. She told him of her encounter with the elderly woman in the elevator and he agreed that he would talk with his patient about the medications. Two weeks later, Erika paid a visit to Dr. Reed's office, dropping off samples of the medications that the older lady had requested. She only had two of the three medications, but it was better than nothing. When she left the building, she felt like she had really done something useful and so she went out and treated herself to dinner at her favorite Mexican restaurant. Dr. Reed had been pretty easy to talk to and he had agreed to pass on samples to those patients in his practice who might benefit from the drugs. Satisfied that she had done the right thing, she ate her dinner and then went home to prepare for work the next day.

As was her usual ritual, she put her suitcase and materials by the door so that she would be ready to start early in the morning. She set up her coffee pot to brew at 5:30 a.m. and then set her alarm clock to wake her at 5:45 a.m. Generally, she got up and showered before having coffee. She grabbed a cup to go and then headed out to the garage with her briefcase and samples. She usually ran into the same few people in the morning on her way to work. The neighbor, Essie Holtz was usually out walking her little dog in the courtyard. Her husband, Mr. Holtz was usually headed to his car at the same time as Erika. He often offered to help her with her bags and she usually refused. There was also Mrs. Taylor who lived across the street from the apartment building. She was usually up sitting on her porch waiting for the newspaper delivery boy.

On this day in particular, Mr. Holtz wasn't heading to his car. Erika noticed that Mrs. Holtz wasn't out walking the dog either. Mrs. Taylor said hello to Erika and waved her over. She told her that Mrs. Holtz had been rushed to the hospital last evening and that Mr. Holtz hadn't yet come home. Erika told Mrs. Taylor to let her know if anything else happened while she was at work today. She wasn't terribly close to her neighbors, but she felt terrible hearing of Mrs. Holtz's illness.

Exactly one week later, Erika heard that Mrs. Holtz had passed away. As it turned out, she'd suffered from a severe heart attack and the doctors hadn't been able to help her. She hadn't been taking her medication because her husband's insurance had run out after he'd retired from his job three months earlier. Erika went to work feeling depressed and just plain disgusted at losing her neighbor. She berated herself for not having been a better friend to the Holtz's and for not checking with Mrs. Holtz to make sure she'd had everything she needed. She could have gotten her some medication if only she'd have asked.

The day didn't improve much when Erika encountered the same old lady in the elevator she had met last week coming from Dr. Reed's office. The old lady didn't speak to her this time and Erika felt an uncomfortable silence as the elevator moved slowly down towards the lobby of the building. Feeling obligated to check, she turned to the older lady and asked her, "Were you able to get your samples from Dr. Reed?"

The old lady gave her a sharp look and then said, "He's never offered me any samples, you probably didn't even give them to him." She didn't say anything else to Erika and when the elevator doors opened, she shuffled past Erika and out the front doors of the building without looking back. She got into a car that was waiting by the entrance to the building. Stung by the exchange, Erika stood there in the elevator as the doors closed again. She waited for a moment and then pushed the button for the lobby so that the doors would open again. When they opened, she was staring down the barrel of a gun. Without a word, the person behind the gun fired and Erika's lifeless body dropped to the floor.

The police were at the building within minutes and the investigation was on. They spoke with everyone in the building and got a list of everyone who had come and gone within the last two hours. They also got the security camera's videotape for the lobby area. The whole thing was just bizarre and as Detective Mathis was finding out, there was absolutely no reason for something like this to have happened. Erika was well-liked by all of the doctors and their office staff. She was generous and had a great personality. She wasn't overbearing and she seemed to genuinely care about the work she was doing.

"It was as if she hoped she was making a difference," said Nancy Atherton, the receptionist at Dr. Powell's office. She cried as she spoke to the police, wiping her tears as she spoke of Erika's visits to their practice.

Another receptionist, Judy Cook said, "I can't imagine who would want to hurt someone like Erika."

The building was shut down for the day while the crime scene was investigated. It was a Friday, so they had the weekend to try and figure out what had happened before people started coming back through on Monday.

What do you think? Who was this elderly woman? Did she have anything at all to do with Erika's murder? If not, then who killed her? **To find out, turn to page 50.**

Out of Focus

Grace Martin was a photographer. She was twenty-three, single and desperate. She had been struggling to make ends meet by working two part-time jobs and taking on assorted freelance projects. One of her part-time jobs was as a waitress for a local family eatery called Mack's. She had been there since high school and was getting tired of the same old routine and had actually given her two weeks notice three times in the last two years in hopes of getting away from the place.

Her other part-time job was as a babysitter for a woman who had a part-time secretarial position for a local tax attorney. Her name was Marguerite Halford. She had two small children, Hattie and Sam. They were three and four, respectively. One evening when Grace was preparing to leave, Marguerite asked her a strange question.

"You're a photographer, right?" she had asked.

"Sure, did you need some pictures taken of the kids?" Grace had asked, hoping for another project.

"Well, not exactly," she said, "It's kind of complicated. Can you hang on for a second while I make sure the kids are still down for their naps? I don't want to talk about it in front of them."

Grace nodded, "Sure, I guess so." She was puzzled. What kind of craziness was she about to hear? Marguerite had already shuffled out of the room to check on the kids and when she came back in, she was carrying what appeared to be women's underwear.

Grace's brow furrowed as she looked at Marguerite's hands. "What's that?" she asked.

"This is why I need pictures," she said nervously.

"I'm sorry; I don't understand what you need…" Grace said, "You need pictures of underwear?"

The color rose in Marguerite's face and she said, "Oh, no, no, not the underwear. It's not mine. That's the problem. I found them here and I'm worried…" She took a deep breath before she continued, "…I'm worried that Ted is having an affair."

Grace's hand flew to her mouth involuntarily. She had been working for Marguerite and her husband Ted for the past three years and this was a little awkward to hear. "Oh, I see," she said.

"Yes, and I was wondering if you had any experience in taking pictures without someone knowing you're taking pictures," Marguerite said. "I need to know who she is."

"Well, I-I don't know, I usually don't do distance shots," Grace started to say. She looked at Marguerite, whose face was flushed and filled with tension. "I mean, I'm not sure I could get a good enough shot with the equipment I've got."

"I'll buy you what you need," Marguerite said, "I need these pictures so that I can go to an attorney. Would you be able to set up somewhere nearby and possibly catch something this weekend?"

"Geez, I guess, I mean, where?" Grace said.

Marguerite had obviously been planning, she answered, "I thought you might be able to set up in the building across the street. I know a lady who lives over there."

The two of them talked about how Grace could get a shot of Ted this weekend. Marguerite was going to visit her mother with the kids this weekend and Ted would be alone at the apartment. Grace could use Marguerite's friend Tess's apartment to set up her camera equipment. It was directly across the street and should be ideal for the kind of shots that Grace would need. Tess was out of town and Marguerite was actually feeding her pets and taking her mail in for her every day, so she had a key to her apartment. This is what had given her the idea in the first place. Marguerite told Grace to go out and get the equipment she needed to take the pictures and to put it on her credit card. She told

Grace that she would pay her $1,000 for pictures that showed anyone other than Ted or family members entering the apartment. It should be easy enough as long as Ted didn't decide to take his escapades on the road instead of bringing his lover to their home.

Grace left Marguerite's apartment feeling low. Although she should have been happy, she felt bad that Ted was deceiving Marguerite. She felt especially bad for the kids. She wasn't sure if she was doing the right thing by trying to help, but she really needed the cash. She reasoned that it would serve a good purpose if Ted really was cheating on Marguerite. If he wasn't, then she could help put Marguerite's mind at ease by reporting that she hadn't seen anything out of the ordinary. Maybe the underwear had been a gift he had bought for her. She hadn't asked Marguerite where she'd found them. Maybe Ted had just hidden them until he could wrap them up for Valentine's Day. These thoughts kept her up all night and when the alarm clock finally went off at 7 a.m. the next morning, she felt as though she hadn't slept at all. Her mind was so cluttered and she had to go to work at Mack's at 9.

She decided to go to work, stop off at the camera store for a telephoto lens for her camera after she finished her shift at 2 p.m. and then head over to Tess's apartment to set up for that night. It was Friday and Marguerite had told her that she and the kids would be heading for her mothers by 1 o'clock. Grace didn't want the kids to see her going into the apartment building, so it was good that they would be gone by the time she got there. Ted worked until around 5 or so and would probably get home by 6. She didn't want to run into him, either. Although it was only five hours, her shift at Mack's went very slowly. She had only six tables during the whole lunch rush and managed to pick up a useless $12 in tips. She left the restaurant at 2 and headed over to the camera equipment store to look for what she needed.

When she talked to the clerk, she asked which lens would work better for long distance shots. She knew, but she needed to talk to someone to take her mind off of what she was preparing to do. The clerk tried to sell her some outrageous piece and she quickly told him she only had half of what that lens cost to spend. He changed his tune and gave her the right lens and she also purchased a tripod and some extra film. She left the store, satisfied with her purchases. These would come in handy after this project. She might even be able to start doing more landscape work. This made the idea of taking pictures of a cheating husband slightly more palatable to Grace.

Grace drove over to the apartment building across from Marguerite's, stopping to get a sandwich on the way. She was relieved to find a parking spot in the lot behind the building. She hadn't wanted to park on the next block and carry all of her equipment down the street. Within fifteen minutes, she had let herself into the apartment and set up the camera. The window in front of the apartment had a direct line of sight to Ted and Marguerite's front door. The apartment building they lived in was more like a condo. Each unit had a door in the front, so there was no question that visitors going in that door would be there for Ted. Once the camera was ready, she took a couple of test shots and then decided to sit down and eat. She looked around the apartment she was in and saw several pictures on the fireplace mantel. They were photos of a Border collie decorated with the usual, cheesy bandana around its neck. These appeared to be the only photographs in the apartment and none of them included a human being. There were no dog bowls around, so Grace assumed that the dog had either passed on or that it was someone else's pet.

As she studied the room, Grace noticed that there was little in the way of clutter. The apartment was tidy and Tess had decorated it very tastefully. There were contemporary white couches arranged around a plain black table. A clear vase with two white roses sat in the middle of the table. The flowers hadn't wilted, so they must have been recent purchases. This made the hair on the back of Grace's neck stand on end. What if Tess wasn't out of town? What if Marguerite had the dates wrong? If Tess came home, how could she explain what she was doing in her apartment with a camera aimed across the street? She didn't know the woman and she was pretty sure that Marguerite hadn't told her what she was up to.

She hurried through her sandwich and threw away her trash. Now that she had herself sufficiently worried, she wasn't sure if she should just pack up and tell Marguerite no one had visited Ted or not. It wasn't quite five o'clock and she really didn't want to stay in the apartment very much longer. She looked out the window and to her surprise, saw that Ted's car was already in the driveway across the street. She hadn't seen him pull up because she had been in the kitchen eating her dinner. As she watched the street, another car pulled up to the curb in front of the condo. She watched in amazement as a woman got out and walked up to the door. Ted opened the door and the woman stepped inside. All this time, Grace had been watching but hadn't thought to snap a picture. She smacked herself in the forehead and decided to go ahead and take a few pictures of the car. Now she would have to wait until the woman came out to get a shot of her.

While she was standing there looking out the window, someone knocked on the apartment door. She froze. She couldn't answer the door so she just stood there and waited for whoever it was to give up and go away. They knocked a few more time and after about five minutes, they must have left. Grace tiptoed over to the door and looked through the peephole. No one was in the hall. She took a deep breath and opened the door. A package had been left in front of the door. She picked it up and took it inside the apartment, forgetting to lock the door behind her. Seconds after she had put the package down on the counter, someone burst through the door and grabbed her from behind. She struggled, but the assailant had her in a choke hold with one hand over her mouth. Moments later, Grace lay on the floor of the kitchen in a pool of blood. She had been stabbed to death and the package she had brought in from the hallway was beside her, unopened and soaked in Grace's blood.

A neighbor had seen someone run down the hallway from Tess's apartment. She had called the police because she knew that Tess wasn't home, but saw that her door was wide open. When the police arrived, they found Grace in the apartment and they assumed that she was Tess. Later, upon closer investigation they discovered that Tess was, in fact, out of town and that the person who had been killed did not live in the building. Grace had no identification with her other than Marguerite's credit card. She had left her purse in the trunk of her car because she'd had so much to carry with the camera equipment. Mistakenly, after checking the name on the card with their database, the police had gone across the street to see if Marguerite was home or if it was her on the kitchen floor of Tess's apartment. Ted had told them that Marguerite was visiting her mother out of town. The police had asked Ted if he could come over and help them identify the body at Tess's apartment.

He had gone without hesitation because he knew Tess and he also knew that she'd had some trouble with an abusive ex-boyfriend in the past. He had been meeting with a client at the condo and he left her there to read over the contracts he'd prepared for the sale of her boat. He was a boat salesman. When he got to the apartment and saw Grace there, he told the police that this was their babysitter. He was puzzled as to why she was here and he noticed that there was a camera set up at the window. The police asked if the camera was Tess's and Ted had told them it was probably Grace's. He told them that she was a photographer, but he wasn't sure why she would be over here with the camera. He didn't think she even knew Tess. The police took the camera as evidence and later found that there were pictures of the car in front of Ted's condo. They also bagged the gift that was beside Grace's body as part of their investigation.

Who killed Grace? Will Marguerite find out what is going on with Ted? Whose underwear were those? To find out, turn to page 51.

The Answers

With One Stone

Marla set the fire at the sanctuary. She called Mrs. McInrude in to talk with her about the vote and while Mrs. McInrude wasn't looking, she turned out the lights and set the fire! Mrs. McInrude perished in the fire. It was Marla who called in to say she was sick, pretending to be Mrs. McInrude.

Marla was having an affair with Dr. Ballast and the two of them boarded a plane shortly after the board meeting where they voted to sell the property. The reason for this: Dr. Ballast was in cahoots with the contractor. He was playing the role of the lone holdout on the vote to make things look good. Actually, the contractor was paying the doctor to make sure the vote went the way it did. The fire was a bonus. Dr. Ballast had no idea the lengths that Marla would go to show him her love. She reinforced the deal by destroying the property and helping him to save face in the community. After all, it was the Ballast Memorial Bird Sanctuary and how would it look if he was willing to sell the property that he developed in his wife's memory?

The two were never found by the police and are currently enjoying a relaxing and decadent lifestyle in the Spain where they work as volunteers in local bird sanctuary.

Board Stiff

Standing behind the gun was Regina, Westmiller's wife. She had long suspected Westmiller was having an affair with someone, but she wasn't sure who. He spent many nights out without as much as a phone call. He talked incessantly about his friend Art and seemed way too interested in what he was doing every evening. She had followed him on several occasions and found him leaving board meetings only to visit Art at his home. She knew that Art was single and that he was a little on the eccentric side, though she had never pegged him as a homosexual. She had changed her mind when she intercepted an e-mail message that Art had sent to her husband earlier in the week. The message had said, "I've got something for you and I think you're going to like it." Mistaking this cryptic message for something flirtatious instead of what it had actually been, a message about the money the two were embezzling, she began planning her revenge.

First, she had paid a homeless man to call the house and threaten her husband. She figured she might be able to scare him into spending less time with his friend by making him think that he was suspected of impropriety. She hadn't actually known that he was trying to take money;

it was just something she had made up. When that didn't seem to work, she had sent him the package with the dead snake hoping that he would be so creeped out that he would confide in her. He hadn't. Instead, he hadn't even mentioned it when he had called her that day. He had called her after his board meeting to say that he wouldn't be home until late. He had some things to take care of at the office.

She was overcome by rage and decided that she would go to Art's house and confront him. She expected to find her husband there, but when she arrived, she found Art dead on the floor. She had hurried out of the house and back to her car, driving away quickly to avoid being spotted. On the way out back to her house, she passed Thornton. He was headed toward Art's house. She had been right about the two of them, she thought to herself as she turned around and headed right back to Art's house. She pulled the dainty little gun she kept for self-defense out of her glove box and headed into the house. She saw Thorn standing over Art's computer, phone in hand. She didn't even give him a chance to explain. She shot him…three times…in the heart.

When the police came, Regina was standing in the hallway. The gun had dropped to her feet after she'd fired the shots. The police quickly handcuffed her and hauled her away. Upon closer investigation, they found that she was only responsible for one of the murders. Coughley had been killed by someone else entirely. Further investigation and an eye witness produced a suspect almost immediately. Mr. Chandler, the Mayfield Family Shelter director had been so enraged by Westmiller's report that the estate money from Mr. Thompson wasn't going to be what they expected that he had gone directly to Coughley's home after the meeting and the two of them had exchanged words. Things had gotten heated and Mr. Chandler had stabbed him, killing him instantly.

Not exactly a professional exchange, but money has a strange effect on some people. Standing there in Coughley's opulent home, Chandler thought about his humble apartment and his measly $30,000 per year salary as shelter director. He looked around at all of the fine things that Coughley had afforded by shuffling money around and his jealousy overtook him. Before he knew it, the knife was in Coughley's chest and he had blood on his hands. He took off, hoping that he hadn't been seen. Unfortunately for Chandler, a homeless man had been hanging around the neighborhood checking the trash cans for things he could resell. He saw everyone that came and went that night and went straight to the police.

Dead Weight

The investigation showed that there were three sets of fingerprints at the crime scene. Darnell, Betsy's and another set. The third set belonged to Sally Metzger. As it unfolded, Sally broke down during the interrogation. Her sister, Beverly Whitford, had killed herself earlier in the year after breaking up with her boyfriend. Her boyfriend was Darnell Wooten and he had broken her heart. Sally decided to play a game with Darnell.

Darnell had already told the others that he would lock up when Sally arrived. They had gone home leaving him and Sally alone in the gym. He had called Betsy while Sally was there listening and when he had finished the conversation, she had whispered something in his ear that had driven him crazy. She lured him into the weight room that night with empty promises of a passionate interlude. Once they were in the weight room and he had laid down on the weight bench, she had injected him with a drug that had caused him to lose consciousness. This she had gotten from her friend, a young doctor whom Darnell had also dated.

As he drifted into unconsciousness, she placed a set of barbells across his throat and began to add weights to either side until she was sure that they were crushing his windpipe. She heard something out front and quietly slipped out of the weight room and hid behind the counter. She saw Betsy heading for the weight room and made her move. By the time she was in her car, Betsy had discovered Darnell.

Unfortunately for Sally, she had been so blinded by the need for revenge; she hadn't taken the necessary precautions to keep from being identified. She hadn't worn gloves because it hadn't occurred to her that they wipe down all of the barbells each evening. She had been too focused on making Darnell pay for her sister's death. Such is the fury of a woman scorned.

An Ounce of Prevention

Erika looked past the barrel of the gun and saw Dr. Reed standing on the other end of it. He said nothing as he fired and then walked quickly away from the scene. He had been Mrs. Holtz's doctor and just two week's ago Mr. Holtz had told him that his neighbor had recommended they try a certain medication. He had mentioned Erika by name and so, the doctor figured she made a point of telling older patients that they needed to pressure their doctors into dealing with drug reps. When he had received the call from her about his other patient, he had been pissed. He was angry at Erika for meddling in his patient affairs. She had no right to pressure him into giving his patients free drugs that might not even help their conditions. He'd always had a negative attitude towards pharmaceutical companies because he felt like they were part of the problem with the health insurance industry. The whole mess cut into his bottom line and he was sick of it. He had been able to stall the investigation by blocking the security cameras in the lobby until he could take care of his problem. The police had discovered his fingerprints on the camera lens and arrested him just three days later.

In the meantime, it was discovered that Marguerite had left the kids at her mother's and came back to town to check up on things. She had arrived at the condo to find a strange woman sitting in her living room reading over contracts. Before the woman could explain what she was doing there, Marguerite had screamed at her telling her to get out of her house. The woman, flustered at the attack, tried to tell Marguerite that Ted had gone across the street to check on something. She was finally able to tell her that the police had asked him to identify a body or something. Marguerite had turned white as a sheet and headed over to the apartment to see what was going on. The coroner's wagon was parked in front of the apartment building where the attendants were loading a body into the back. She asked them who it was and they told her that they couldn't give details. She started to go into the apartment building, but was stopped by an officer at the door.

"What happened here?" she asked, "My husband was brought over here to identify a body, I think?"

"Who are you, ma'am?" the officer asked her.

"I'm Marguerite Halford, I live across the street," she said, pointing to her condo.

The officer radioed someone and then told her that she could go on up. When she got to the apartment, she saw the blood on the kitchen floor. She saw Ted standing there talking with the police officers and she ran toward him. He hugged her and then asked her what she was doing there. "Where are the kids?" he asked. He hadn't wanted them to know what had happened to Grace. She told him that she had gotten all the way to her mother's and that Sam had been crying for his blanket. She told her mother that she would get the blanket and come back so that they could spend the rest of the weekend with her. Ted thought this was strange, but he let it pass.

"Did Grace know Tess?" he asked Marguerite.

"I don't know, I don't think so," she said, trying to conceal her nervousness.

"The victim had one of your credit cards on her when we found her," an officer told Marguerite.

"One of my credit cards?" Marguerite asked, feigning surprise, "What was she doing with that?"

"Good question," the officer said. "How long had she worked for you?"

"Oh, she's been with us about three years," she answered.

"Did you ever have a problem with anything coming up missing before?" he asked.

Marguerite was silent for a moment and then said, "No, not that I'm aware of. You don't think she stole the card. Surely there's an explanation."

"If there is, we'll probably never know it now," the officer said, shaking his head.

The police officer gave Ted and Marguerite permission to leave the scene and the two of them headed back across the street to their condo. Marguerite called her mother to let her know what had happened and that she would be back as soon as she could. Ted called his client, who had left the minute Marguerite had gone across the street. He needed to smooth things over with her so that the boat sale wouldn't fall through. They had sat there, looking at each other for several moments when Ted said, "What the hell was she doing over there?"

Marguerite just shook her head. She said, "She was such a sweet girl, who could have done this to her?"

The two of them decided that Marguerite should go back to stay with the kids and that Ted would join them tomorrow afternoon once he had finished working on the boat deal from earlier this evening. They spent the next few days trying to figure out how to tell the kids that Grace wouldn't be coming back. After that, Marguerite started looking for a new sitter. She and Ted had been getting along very well and she had since given up on the notion that he had been cheating on her. It was still nagging at her a little, but she wasn't as worried about proving it now.

Weeks later, the investigation revealed that the killer had been female. The fingerprints on the blood-soaked package had belonged to none other than Marguerite Halford. When she was interrogated, she revealed to the police that she had found evidence that Grace had been sleeping with her husband, Ted. The evidence she was referring to was the pair of lacy underwear that she had shown Grace just weeks before. She had talked the girl into taking the pictures knowing that there would be no visitors because she thought Grace had been having an affair with him while she was working at their home. Knowing that Tess's ex-boyfriend James was still a known threat and that people would most likely think that he had broken in and killed Grace by mistake she had taken the kids to her mother's at noon that day and then came back to Tess's apartment. She figured that once she was alone in the apartment with her, she would confront Grace about her relationship with Ted.

The gift had contained the pair of underwear that she assumed Grace had left at her house. A small card had been tucked inside and it had read, "I know it was you, bitch." She had planned this big elaborate confrontation where Grace would open the package and then she would attack her, but when it came down to it, she had lost her nerve and acted out of rage. She had planned to take the camera and the gift with her when she left the apartment, but she had been so flustered that she ran out of the apartment without the camera or the gift. She was further enraged when she realized that there was a strange car outside her condo and that it appeared that Ted had a different woman in her home that night. She had been wrong on all counts.

Grace hadn't been having an affair with Ted. The underwear had in fact, been a gift for Marguerite. Ted had wanted to spice up their love life by buying her some fancy lingerie. He hadn't wrapped them because he had wanted to slip them into her dresser drawer along with a rose on Valentine's Day. He had tucked them under the mattress on his side of their bed thinking that she'd never look there. It just so happened that she was flipping the mattress when she discovered them. Poor Grace had been killed for no reason. Her instincts about Ted had been right; he wasn't having an affair at all.

Marguerite was sentenced to life in prison and Ted, well; he started dating his neighbor, Tess just six months after Marguerite went to jail.

www.ingramcontent.com/pod-product-compliance
Lightning Source LLC
LaVergne TN
LVHW050945080826
845145LV00004B/1420

* 9 7 8 0 6 1 5 1 9 1 3 2 4 *